WHEN YOU ARE SAD

Henry Says Good-Bye

EDWARD T. WELCH
Editor

JOE HOX
Illustrator

Henry Hedgehog woke to the sound of his little sister, Halle, reading stories to Mama and Papa—stories with happy endings. Henry didn't care for happy endings—not right now. Nothing felt happy without his ladybug, Lila.

As he got dressed for school, Henry thought about the first time he met Lila.

He had just come home from school, when he saw a spotted wing case on the screen door. Lila smiled, fluttered her wings, and flew right to Henry's paw. They became instant friends.

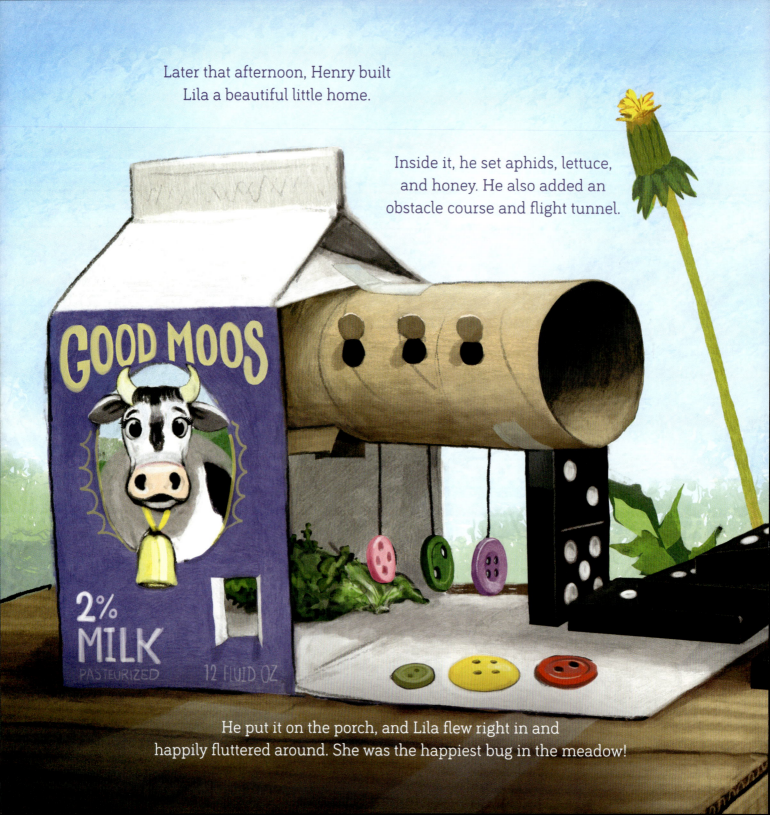

Later that afternoon, Henry built Lila a beautiful little home.

Inside it, he set aphids, lettuce, and honey. He also added an obstacle course and flight tunnel.

He put it on the porch, and Lila flew right in and happily fluttered around. She was the happiest bug in the meadow!

Several days later, Henry asked Lila,
"Would you like to come to school with me today?
All of my friends bring their pets, so if you come,
you can make new friends, too!

You can ride in my backpack!"

Lila fluttered her wings as if to say yes.

Soon, Lila had a whole new host of friends. She met honey bees, butterflies, dragonflies, and even a praying mantis! Each day at recess, the pets outdid each other in performing flying tricks.

They flew in circles,
did barrel rolls,
and raced each other.

They had the best time! At the end of recess, each pet returned to their backpack for a nap.

But, one particular day, Lila wanted to stay out of her backpack.
She teetered on the edge of the backpack pocket,
just waiting for the right moment to escape.

And so it happened—
right in the middle of
Miss Minnick's math lesson.

Lila sprung out of the backpack and into the air.
She put on a spectacular aerobatic show.

Lila spun around the class, creating lines, loops, and rolls!
She even did a hammerhead.
The other pets woke from their naps and peeked out of their backpacks.

Lila was as free as ever—
flying, looping, soaring.

She was having the time of her life—
that is, until she accidentally landed
on Miss Minnick's forehead!

Miss Minnick yelped, hollered, and swung around backwards, until she finally cupped Lila in her hands.

She said, "Gotcha, Lila! You know the rules: pets stay in their backpacks for class."

Although Lila never again escaped during class, everyone always remembered her spectacular show.

But one day Henry noticed that Lila's spots were fading and she seemed tired.

Mama said, "Our little bug isn't feeling well today. Why don't we let her rest. I'll keep an eye on her while you're at school."

Henry missed Lila so much that day, especially at recess when all the other pets were playing together.

As soon as school ended, Henry rushed home.

When he saw Mama's face, he knew something was wrong. She said, "I'm so sorry, sweetie. Lila's spots continued to fade throughout the day. This afternoon our sweet Lila bug died."

As Henry listened to Mama's words, his throat swelled and his eyes watered. His quills raised and bristled. He felt speechless and afraid.
He was stunned and silent.

That night, Henry didn't want dinner. When Mama and Papa said goodnight and closed his bedroom door, he rolled into a prickly ball and cried. He didn't understand why this had to happen—why to Lila, and why to him. He felt so alone. He couldn't imagine facing tomorrow and telling his friends— let alone seeing them with their pets.

Then he noticed Lila's flight tunnel on the floor and cried himself to sleep.

The more Henry thought about how much he missed Lila, the less he wanted to go to school.

He didn't want to talk to anyone! He wanted to curl up in a ball and hide.

When Mama said she'd made his favorite blueberry buckle breakfast, he replied, "I'm not hungry." When she said, "You really should eat before school," he rushed toward the door, brushing past Halle and knocking over her blocks.

He didn't notice that Halle was also sad.
She loved Lila too.

Henry was quiet at school that day.

When his friends invited him to play at recess, he told them he didn't want to play and instead he sat by himself.

Henry's friend Buster said, "We heard about Lila. We're so sorry." But all Henry could think of was that his friends still had their pets. He watched them continue with their games and stories. Sadly he thought, *I won't ever have any new Lila stories*.

Later that evening at home, Papa said, "Henry, can we talk?"

Henry said, "I don't want to talk! Nothing can be fixed. Nothing can make her come back."

Papa said, "Separation from those we love is painful. It hurts. Have any of your friends lost a pet? Were you able to talk with them today?"

Henry sadly replied, "I'm the only one." And then he started to cry.

"I remember when my pet, Sarah Spider, died.
I was so angry and confused." said Papa.

"So, what did you do?"

"Grandpa encouraged me to share my feelings with God and others. He reminded me that it was okay to cry and that God's people in the Great Book often cried over their sadness. The Great Book says that God keeps a record of our tears.

Here's a verse for you to put in your back pocket."
Papa handed Henry a little piece of paper and he read:

You keep track of all my sorrows. You have collected all my tears in your bottle. You have recorded each one in your book. Psalm 56:8

Papa continued, "Remember that God cares about your sadness and is so close to you that he can count all of your tears!"
Henry looked up. He was still crying, but he didn't feel so alone.

Papa said, "I wonder if it might be good for us to remember Lila with your friends. We could invite them over to share stories and to thank God that we got to know Lila. Does that sound like a good plan?"

Henry replied, "That might be nice."

When Henry invited his friends, they were more than glad to come! They loved Lila, and they also loved him. He didn't feel so angry anymore that they still had their pets. He was thankful they were coming to remember Lila with him.

Papa, Mama, Halle, and Henry decorated the backyard. They hung red and black balloons and covered a table with a red cloth and black polka-dots.

On the table they set pictures of Lila—in her little home, in the grass, and at school.

Once their friends arrived, Papa said, "Thank you all for coming to remember Lila. She was a wonderful friend and pet, and we're glad you're here. Henry will begin by sharing a few words. Please feel free to share your memories as well."

Henry began, "Lila was a special bug. The first day I met her, I loved her. From her aerobatics to her silly tricks, she was always making me smile. I'm really going to miss her. I'll miss holding her, laughing at her tricks, and going to school with her every day."

One by one, Henry's friends shared their own stories.

Buster shared about Lila's epic flight in Miss Minnick's class. Tori shared about the time Lila snuck away during recess. And Jax shared about the time she tickled his neck with her wings.

I know, Henry, that you are so sad today, but I want to tell you about a day that is coming when there will be no more tears or goodbyes. That day will be when we go to heaven to be with Jesus. The Great Book says that on that day, Jesus 'will wipe every tear from our eyes. There will be no more death, sadness, crying, or pain.' Everyone who trusts in Jesus and asks him for forgiveness will be with him forever. We know this is true because Jesus rose from the dead and is alive right now!"

Papa distributed cards with those words from the Great Book. Each card had a picture of Lila on the front.

Mama hugged Henry. She said, "You know we all miss Lila. I know that Halle is sad too. The Great Book tells us that God is our merciful Father and the source of all comfort. He comforts us in all our troubles so that we can comfort others."

Then Henry pictured his sister, Halle. He remembered how she also loved Lila. She used to watch Lila when Henry had soccer practice. And she was always willing to help clean her cage. He also remembered angrily rushing past her and knocking over her blocks. He never thought of how she might also be sad.

Henry prayed, "Please help me see others who are hurting. Help me to comfort them with the same comfort you are giving me."

Then he saw Halle on the front porch, building a block city.

He said, "I'm sorry that I was mean to you when I was sad about Lila."

Halle looked up, smiled, and said, "That's okay, Henry, I know you were upset. Do you want to help me build?"

Helping Your Child with Sadness

We hate to see our children sad, but we also know there are many griefs to come, so now is a rich opportunity to help our children grow in the midst of sorrow. Many of us wish we had the same opportunity when we were younger to learn about how Jesus helps us in our sadness.

Henry has experienced loss. In this story, he lost a pet ladybug, but the loss could be a friendship, a friend, a relative, a precious toy, or even a blanket that has been a lifelong comfort. Grief and sadness are our natural response to losing something important to us. Here are some truths from the Bible to share as you talk with your child about a loss.

1. **The Lord never minimizes our loss and grief.** God never tells us our sadness is unimportant. While it is true we can love things on earth more than we love Jesus, you simply will not find any Scripture that minimizes a loss. The Lord does not adjust his compassion based on its street value, as if plastic toys receive 20 percent of his compassion and comfort, small pets 40 percent, large pets 60 percent, and family members 100 percent. His compassion is not based on the merits of the item lost, but on his love for the person who grieves. Psalm 10:14 says, "God, you see the problems of people in trouble. You take note of their pain. You do something about it" (NIRV).

2. **Speak of your own sadness, invite your child to speak, and be patient.** You feel your child's loss because you love him or her. And since grief is intended to be spoken, you will put your sadness into words. That is how relationships work in God's family. We speak our grief to him, and we speak it to those we love and who love us. So many of the psalms teach us how to speak our troubles to the Lord rather than keep them to ourselves. "O my people, trust in him at all times. Pour out your heart to him, for God is our refuge" (Psalm 62:8).

   Children might need time before they can talk about their feelings. Grief can feel very alone at first—no one, it seems, could ever understand. Words seem to fail. But be patient. You can probably remember times when you wanted to be alone in your grief, at least for a little while. Along the way you can, like the psalms, speak a few words that could help your child find words for the swirling feelings within.

3. **Why?** A younger child might not ask this question, but older children do, and you probably do. There are many ways to answer it, yet no answer will fully satisfy. It is better to rephrase the question into one that is even more important: "Does God care?" Now we get to the very heart of God's response to grief. Remind your child of the following truths (and yourself as well).

4 God is close. He is not a distant king who hears reports from his ambassadors. He is the one who personally comes close to us by his Spirit. Remind your child of these promises:

Never will I leave you, never will I forsake you. (Hebrews 13:5 NIV)

The LORD is close to the brokenhearted. He saves those whose spirits have been crushed. (Psalm 34:18 ICB)

God hears and remembers. His greatness is such that he is attentive to each individual sheep, and what he hears he remembers. "You keep track of all my sorrows. You have collected all my tears in your bottle. You have recorded each one in your book" (Psalm 56:8). This verse is a request, but it is a request based on God's promise that he hears and remembers. Our tears themselves are placed in the royal records, never erased from the King's attention. He will remember long after grief fades.

God comforts. Adults can be close. They can hear and remember, but they don't necessarily have the power to do too much. God, however, acts. When he hears, he is doing something. When he remembers, he is busy on our behalf. It is Jesus himself who will comfort. He is the one who knows grief. He is the God of compassion and mercy (Exodus 34:6). He is the Lamb who attends to our grief. "For the Lamb on the throne will be their Shepherd. He will lead them to springs of life-giving water. And God will wipe every tear from their eyes" (Revelation 7:17). That's a picture of our heavenly future for all who trust in Jesus. But, right now Jesus is joining heaven and earth in himself, so we should expect features of heaven to break through into today. With this in mind, keep a look out for how and when Jesus wipes away some of the tears. The image is beautiful—Jesus is close, listening, filled with compassion—so close he touches and wipes away tears in a way that relieves some of the pain of loss. All this is a result of how he has forgiven our sin in his death, and we, in response, have said, "Thank you," and put our trust in him. Now there is nothing that can separate us from him. Remind your child of this great truth. Invite him or her to trust Jesus. Let your child see you living a life of trust in Jesus as you face your own losses.

5 We comfort. As tears subside and children know a little more of God's comfort, they have a growing soft spot for other people who are sad and grieved. Now they can do something. They can express their sorrow for someone's loss. They can remind others of God's comfort, just as Henry did with Lila at the end of the book. Paul puts it like this, "Praise be to the God and Father of our Lord Jesus Christ. God is the Father who is full of mercy. And he is the God of all comfort. He comforts us every time we have trouble, so that we can comfort others when they have trouble. We can comfort them with the same comfort that God gives us. We share in the many sufferings of Christ. In the same way, much comfort comes to us through Christ" (2 Corinthians 1:3-5 ICB).

6 Keep heaven in view. When we trust in Jesus and ask him for forgiveness for our sins, heaven comes into view. There will be a day when sadness, crying, and death is ended. This is how the Bible describes that day, "I heard a loud shout from the throne, saying, 'Look, God's home is now among his people! He will live with them, and they will be his people. God himself will be with them. He will wipe every tear from their eyes, and there will be no more death or sorrow or crying or pain. All these things are gone forever.' And the one sitting on the throne said, 'Look, I am making everything new!'" (Revelation 21:3-5). As you walk with your children through sadness and loss, keep heaven in view and remember together that a day is coming when there will be no more tears and sorrow. Share the gospel with your children and invite them to turn from going their own way and put their trust in Jesus. Then, even at a young age, they can become ambassadors who pray and care for others. Even children can taste something of the sufferings of Jesus, participate in his comfort, and share the hope of heaven and the good news of Jesus with their friends.

"O my people, trust in him at all times. Pour out your heart to him, for God is our refuge."

Psalm 62:8

Story creation by Jocelyn Flenders, a homeschooling mother, writer, and editor living in suburban Philadelphia. A graduate of Lancaster Bible College with a background in intercultural studies and counseling, the Good News for Little Hearts series is her first published work for children.

New Growth Press, Greensboro, NC 27404
Text copyright © 2019 by Edward T. Welch
Illustration copyright © 2019 by New Growth Press

All rights reserved. No part of this publication may be reproduced, stored in a retrieval system, or transmitted in any form by any means, electronic, mechanical, photocopy, recording, or otherwise, without the prior permission of the publisher, except as provided by USA copyright law.

Scripture quotations marked NIV are taken from THE HOLY BIBLE, NEW INTERNATIONAL VERSION®, NIV® Copyright © 1973, 1978, 1984, 2011 by Biblica, Inc.® Used by permission. All rights reserved worldwide. Scripture quotations marked NIrV are taken from the Holy Bible, NEW INTERNATIONAL READER'S VERSION®. Copyright © 1996, 1998 Biblica. All rights reserved throughout the world. Used by permission of Biblica.

Cover/Interior Design and Typesetting: Trish Mahoney, themahoney.com

ISBN: 978-1-948130-78-3

LCCN 2019945099

Printed in India

28 27 26 25 24 23 22 21   3 4 5 6 7

GOOD NEWS FOR LITTLE HEARTS

Back Pocket Bible Verses

The LORD is close to the brokenhearted. He saves those whose spirits have been crushed.

Psalm 34:18 (ICB)

You keep track of all my sorrows. You have collected all my tears in your bottle. You have recorded each one in your book.

Psalm 56:8

"Look, God's home is now among his people! He will live with them, and they will be his people. God himself will be with them. He will wipe every tear from their eyes, and there will be no more death or sorrow or crying or pain. All these things are gone forever." And the one sitting on the throne said, "Look, I am making everything new!"

Revelation 21:3–5

Praise be to the God and Father of our Lord Jesus Christ. God is the Father who is full of mercy. And he is the God of all comfort. He comforts us every time we have trouble, so that we can comfort others when they have trouble. We can comfort them with the same comfort that God gives us. We share in the many sufferings of Christ. In the same way, much comfort comes to us through Christ.

2 Corinthians 1:3–5 (ICB)

GOOD NEWS FOR LITTLE HEARTS

Back Pocket Bible Verses

WHEN YOU ARE SAD

WHEN YOU ARE SAD

GOOD NEWS FOR LITTLE HEARTS

GOOD NEWS FOR LITTLE HEARTS

WHEN YOU ARE SAD

WHEN YOU ARE SAD

GOOD NEWS FOR LITTLE HEARTS

GOOD NEWS FOR LITTLE HEARTS